THE GIRL
WHO SPUN GOLD

VIRGINIA HAMILTON

THE GIRL WHO SPUN GOLD

illustrated by

LEO & DIANE DILLON

THE BLUE SKY PRESS • AN IMPRINT OF SCHOLASTIC INC. • NEW YORK

THE BLUE SKY PRESS

Text copyright © 2000 by Virginia Hamilton

Illustrations copyright © 2000 by Leo & Diane Dillon

All rights reserved.

No part of this publication may be reproduced or stored in a retrieval system

or transmitted in any form or by any means, electronic, mechanical, photocopying,

recording, or otherwise, without written permission of the publisher.

For information regarding permission, please write to: Permissions Department,

The Blue Sky Press, an imprint of Scholastic Inc.,

555 Broadway, New York, New York 10012.

The Blue Sky Press is a registered trademark of Scholastic Inc.

Library of Congress catalog card number: 99-086365

ISBN 0-590-47378-6

10 9 8 7 6 5 4 3 2 1   0/0 01 02 03 04

Printed in Singapore   46

First printing, September 2000

For Leigh and Jaime
V. H.

For Bonnie, Kathy, Angela, and Lee: thank you
L. & D. D.

THERE BE THIS TALE told about a tiny fellow who could hide in a foot of shade amid old trees. All that most could see of him was the way he sparkled.

Some say he wore a pointy hat; he had one true leg. The other leg stood straight-out stiff and was made of wood. He had a long tail. He could fly through the air—tis true! He had magic. And when the shade danced with flecks of gold, it was the little fellow, himself—Lit'mahn—going about his mischief. Anybody and everybody old, like the trees, knew how he could appear and disappear, and they knew enough to stay out of his shade.

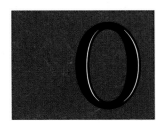NE DAY, young Big King came riding amidst the trees. And just then, Lit'mahn was hiding in the shade, watching a lovely girl spinning plain thread. She and her mama were laughing and talking loud when Big King turned his horses and stopped before them.

Says he, "Here! What's all this noise in my kingdom?"

Well, the mama, thinking fast, says, "Oh, great Big King, my daughter is spinning a whole field of finest golden thread to make cloth for his Highest. And we are so happy, we are rejoicing about it, don't cha know."

"Well, if that's true," said the king, "I will have to marry your daughter, who is very beautiful, and she will be my queen."

Quashiba was the daughter's name. She was upset at her mama's terrible fib. For she spun only the plainest thread. And how would she weave a whole field of cloth? Shyly now, Quashiba looked up from her spinning wheel to smile on the handsome king. And he smiled back.

SOON, A WEDDING DAY was arranged for them. Oh, it came quickly! There was cake and all so good food, baking bread, roasted goat, and chickens cooking. For a while, the mama forgot what she had said about the golden thread, she was so very happy for her daughter.

And the whole kingdom was decked with flowers. And all turned out for a splendid wedding day. The two got married, they did. Everybody called out their names: "Big King! Queen Quashiba!" It was as if the sound of fresh wind rolled out of the hills and washed over the land. "Big King! Queen Quashiba! Hooray!"

WELL, BIG KING had to become even bigger than he needed to be. Being young, he went too far. He told Quashiba, said, "You can have everything," spreading his arms wide. "You can have fine robes, gowns, and friends to call upon you. But after the year ends and one day more, you will start spinning golden thread. You hear me? You must start weaving me three whole rooms of golden things!" The king left her there with her mother.

"Oh, law!" cried the mama. "You hear that, Queenie Quashi?" (That's what she called her own sweet daughter.) "I am so sorry for what I said. Oh, I'm afraid for you!"

"Never you mind, Mama," Queenie Quashi said. "Never you sorrow, my dearie-dear. You will see. Big King-mahn will forget about it, the golden stuff he wants me to spin be such a long time coming."

**A**LL WAS BEST and good for a year and a day. Queen Quashiba had footmen and headmen; she had pie-makers and cake-bakers. She made her handmaids spin the threads. All bad was forgotten. Until, one day, Big King came and took her to a room as large as a playing field.

"Better have this room spun full of golden thread and cloth and things by dawn," said he. "Else you'll stay cooped up in here forever and a year!" He padlocked the iron door against her.

Tears ran down Quashiba's face, she was so sad, and afraid, trembling all over, for she only knew how to spin plain thread. But, oh, shhh! Hearing a noise, she peered around. And, there! A tiny man came floating! He was all over ugly, for true! He grinned at Quashiba. He bowed grandly to her, standing on the air. And tipped the tall, green hat he wore.

It was Lit'mahn, himself, the tiny shade fellow. His wooden leg never bended. He wore striped trousers. And he had a long tail that swung this-away and that-away. Poor Quashiba was more frightened than ever.

LIT'MAHN SPOKE: "Girl, what's the matter, you?" Said kindly enough.

So Queen Quashiba quieted her fear and told him her own true name and all the good, and the bad, that had happened to her.

"I'll help you with making golden things," he said. "But you must guess my whole name."

"And if I can't guess it?" Queen Quashiba asked.

"You have three nights to try, and three chances each night. And if you can't guess my name by the final night and the last chance, then I will make you tiny, just like me. I will carry you off to live in my shade!"

Queen Quashiba couldn't stand to be near the little fellow. But sweetly, she said, "I thank you kindly! I will be naming you within the three nights and with the chances that you've given me."

"Good!" cried Lit'mahn. He began singing and twirling his tail, and flying round and round the room-big-as-a-field. Quashiba got so sleepy with all his sashaying up and down that she yawned twice, and fell to slumber.

B Y ' N ' B Y , she awoke. All was dark, with the moonlight creeping through her windows. Lit'mahn was right there, bowing and grinning. The room-big-as-a-field soon shone, full of golden thread and cloth and things to the ceiling!

And Lit'mahn spoke then, softly: "Queenie Quashi, what's my name?"

Wide-eyed Quashiba thought hard. "Your name be Septimus," she said at last.

"No-a!" shouted he.

"Then your name must be Obidiah!"

"No-a!" Lit'mahn laughed the hat off his head. Did! Put it back on.

Queen Quashiba thought about it and thought about it. "Jemajama!" she shouted.

Lit'mahn hollered loud, "No-a! Oh, no, no, no-ahhhh!" He doubled over laughing, "Hee-d'hee-hee!" He leaped up and flew out of there.

Dawn light, and Big King came and unlocked Quashiba's room. There was all the gold cloth, bright as the sun. Big King was so happy he kissed Quashiba's hand. Later he led her into another room. "Fill this room with gold!" he commanded. And he padlocked her in and left her there, all alone.

QUEEN QUASHIBA stood, feeling bad, when there came the little man through the open window. He brought her food and water. And while she tried to eat, he flew as easily as a feather floating. Bowing, he grinned and twirled. It made Quashiba so dizzy she pushed the food away. Poor child, she fell asleep in her chair, just before the night came down.

Later, it was, when she came wide awake at some sound. Lit'mahn was there, showing his toothy grin. The room was filled clear up, clear down, and all around with gold thread and cloth and things. There were gold mirrors, and they showed Lit'mahn made of winking gold flecks.

"Good evening, my Queenie. Now what is my name?" Lit'mahn asked her.

Quashiba said right back: "Your name is Nicholas."

He said, "No-a!"

"Then it must be Nehemiah!"

And he said again, "No-a! Oh, no-ahhhhh!" Sounded like sighing.

Quashiba frowned and said, "Nebercouldgethim!"

"No-a!" The little fellow-mahn laughed and laughed. And rose up and flew away.

IG KING came, saw the second room full of golden stuff. He was so happy he asked his poor wife to have supper with him. The servants brought a feast of hog and apples with plantains, fish and coconuts, red beans and rice.

Queen Quashiba was so happy to be out of that room. Big King looked happy, too. He was proud of her, he said. "So smart are you to know to spin golden threads!" They ate and laughed and talked. He told her about something he'd seen.

"I'm out hunting wild hogs this day," he said. "In the woods, I am, and I come upon a big hole in the ground at the foot of a tree. And down in this hole there stands a funny little mahn with a wooden leg and striped trousers on, an' wearing a tall green hat. He has a tail, and he's dancin' on his best leg and singing a song. I sat very still to listen:

"'My name be Lit'mahn, Lit'mahn,

Hey-o, oohum, Lit'mahn, Lit'mahn, be me.'"

Quashiba's eyes opened wide. Her mouth formed an *O* in surprise.

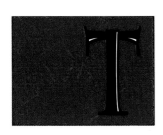

HE KING had to laugh. "Well, he was a funny fellow. He had more to sing about, and he did!"

"What?" Quashiba asked breathlessly.

"This Lit'mahn, he spoke on about himself," said Big King.

My name be Lit'mahn, I am not tall but am quite short, sang he.
Dear Mother said to me, 'You are the magic one.
My forever favorite, LIT'MAHN BITTYUN!'

"Lit'mahn Bittyun!" whispered the queen. "Awh, law!"

"Comical little fellow he was, for true," said the king.

After they had eaten, Big King told her, "Last time, Quashiba, just one more room of gold, please now. Good night," he said, and he padlocked the door.

But Quashiba wouldn't say a word. Angry, she was, at the king, for treating her so. Angry also at the creature of magic, Lit'mahn Bittyun!

**F**OR IN the room, soon as the door was locked, Lit'mahn flew through the open window to her side. He grinned. He bowed and said, "This be your last chance, my Queenie. You better get my name right, or I am going to make you an itty-bitty Quashi, tinier than me!"

He danced around her, and he sang and twirled his tail. And Queen Quashiba fell fast asleep on the floor.

She woke up soon, oh yes. Of course, the room was full to bursting with golden stuffs.

Lit'mahn was right there, sitting on top of the high gold pile. Spoke he, "Queenie Quashi, guess you well this time. You only have three chances. If you don't know my name, you will be forever shaded and ever so small!" His tail whirled round and round so fast, Quashiba lost sight of it.

And she said, "Your name is Squashimup!"

"No-a!" And tail, whizzing through the air! "Two more guesses!"

"Your name must be...no...must be Teardowndoor!"

"No-a, it's not! You better think good this one last time!"

**A**ND SO Quashiba thought good and strong. She put hands to hips and reared back. She told him, "Your name be...be... *Lit'mahn Bittyun*! Yes! The name your mother gave you, you ugly, silly, tiny thing!"

Ah! See! Lit'mahn gave out a screech so loud, it turned the moon around. The hat jumped off his head. His ears fell off!

"POP-OP!" he goes, in a million bitty flecks of gold that flowed into the night and disappeared.

Real loud noise, was Lit'mahn Bittyun going. He sounded like hot grease in a wet skillet, as all of him vanished in the dark.

There was left a scent of burning feathers, that was all.

QUEEN QUASHIBA would not talk to Big King for three long years and three long fields full of him saying, "Forgive me, my Queen Quashiba! I was so greedy to ask for golden things. I have buried every padlock in our kingdom!"

And that's the story told. They say Queen Quashiba finally forgave Big King. And they lived fairly happily ever after.

But never again did anyone old like the trees see sparkly Lit'mahn Bittyun in the shade. Some elders say he comes near, still, dancing and floating above our heads. And when is that?

Don't cha know! Each time, they say, when his tale be told.

ABOUT THE STORY IN THIS BOOK

The folktale of a cruel little man who helps a woman spin thread or straw or flax into skeins of gold is a well-loved tale with variants around the world.

In England, the little man's name, Tom Tit Tot, is the title of one story, and in another story, "Duffy and the Devil," he *is* the Devil and has no other name. In Germany, the little man's name is also the title of the best-known little-man story ever, "Rumpelstiltskin."

The Girl Who Spun Gold is my version of a West Indian variant of the little-man tale entitled "Mr. Titman," meaning "little man," from a collection by Pamela Colman Smith, published in 1899 by R.H. Russell, New York. As with several African American variants, the West Indian variant is told in a difficult, so-called black dialect.

In *The Girl Who Spun Gold* I have translated the language into a far simpler colloquial style, which is easy to read aloud, and is a truer reflection of a lilting West Indian speech pattern, then and now.

—VIRGINIA HAMILTON

ABOUT THE PAINTINGS IN THIS BOOK

Knowing the difficulty of painting with metallic paint as well as the difficulty of reproducing gold, we still chose to use it, for the story itself revolved around the concept of gold. The art was done with acrylic paint on acetate, over-painted with gold paint. The gold borders were created using gold leaf.

—LEO & DIANE DILLON

The artwork in *The Girl Who Spun Gold* was reproduced in four-color process with gold as a fifth color. The book was printed on one-hundred-pound Nymolla Matte paper, and each illustration was spot-varnished. Color separations were made by Digicon Imaging Inc., Buffalo, New York, and the book was printed and bound by Tien Wah Press, Singapore, with production supervision by Angela Biola and Alison Forner. The book was designed by Leo & Diane Dillon and Kathleen Westray.